Maggie

Diary Two

Other books by
Ann M. Martin

P.S. Longer Letter Later
(written with Paula Danziger)
Leo the Magnificat
Rachel Parker, Kindergarten Show-off
Eleven Kids, One Summer
Ma and Pa Dracula
Yours Turly, Shirley
Ten Kids, No Pets
Slam Book
Just a Summer Romance
Missing Since Monday
With You and Without You
Me and Katie (the Pest)
Stage Fright
Inside Out
Bummer Summer

THE KIDS IN MS. COLMAN'S CLASS series
BABY-SITTERS LITTLE SISTER series
THE BABY-SITTERS CLUB mysteries
THE BABY-SITTERS CLUB series
CALIFORNIA DIARIES series

California Diaries #8

Maggie

Diary Two

Ann M. Martin

SCHOLASTIC INC.
New York Toronto London Auckland Sydney

*The author gratefully acknowledges
Jeanne Betancourt
for her help in
preparing this manuscript.*

No part of this publication may be reproduced in whole or in part, or stored in a retrieval system, or transmitted in any form or by any means, electronic, mechanical, photocopying, recording, or otherwise, without written permission of the publisher. For information regarding permission, write to Scholastic Inc., Attention: Permissions Department, 555 Broadway, New York, NY 10012.

ISBN 0-590-02383-7

Copyright © 1998 by Ann M. Martin.
All rights reserved. Published by Scholastic Inc.
CALIFORNIA DIARIES is a trademark of Scholastic Inc.

12 11 10 9 8 7 6 5 4 3 2 1   8 9/9 0 1 2 3/0

Printed in the U.S.A.   40

First Scholastic printing, August 1998

Monday 7/13
2:30 P.M.

Breakfast: Small bowl of cornflakes w/skim milk, black coffee (no sugar).
Lunch: ½ tuna sandwich (NO mayo), diet soda, 1 apple (small).
Goal: Don't eat between meals.
Weight: 103½ lbs.
Goal: 90 lbs.

Starting today I, Maggie Blume, vow to write down every bite that goes into my mouth.

I have to face facts. I am one of those people who gain weight if they eat five peanuts. I'll have to watch what I eat for the rest of my life. I might as well start now.

Everyone tells me I don't need to lose weight. Amalia says it. Ducky says it. Dawn says it. They say I have a great body. They are WRONG WRONG WRONG. They don't see me when I'm in my underwear. They don't see me when I'm on the scale. They think I'm thin, but I'm FAT. Thirteen pounds. That's all I need to lose.

I was really smart about lunch. I waited until two o'clock to eat. I'm noticing that when I eat slowly I enjoy my food more. The apple was so good. Clean and fresh. No fat.

Someone brought a dozen donuts into the office kitchen this morning. I was nauseous just looking at them. Grease, fat, calories! Croissants are just as bad. They're full of butter.

This afternoon I have to make 35 copies of the script for the next film Dad's producing. They finally settled on a title for it — *Never.*

During my first week of work Dad asked me to read the script for *Never.* "Write up a summary of the plot and tell me what you think of it," he said. "I value your opinion."

He doesn't really care what I think about the script. He just wants me to feel like I'm part of his team.

I read it.

I think *Never* is a perfect name for this

movie. As in, "Never go see it." But I didn't write that in my "review." I told Dad what I knew he wanted to hear — "Exciting and suspenseful." It would just have caused tension between us if I told him what I really think.

It's so weird. Hundreds of people are working and spending zillions of dollars on a movie that is basically dumb. Car chases and violence. All that money wasted.

I know Dad isn't always proud of the kinds of films he makes. But he is proud of being a big success.

His movies make money.

He likes his money and all the things it can buy.

Including all the things that keep the Blume family going.

Sometimes I feel like a hypocrite when I think about Dad like this. I live in the big fancy house. Swim in the pool. Wear the nice clothes (though they don't look so nice on me). And have all kinds of advantages.

But working for my father is NOT one of them. At work he is Mr. Phony. Mr. Schmooze.

Mr. I'll-kill-you-with-kindness-but-you-have-to-do-it-my-way.

We see that side of Dad at home sometimes. But at Blume Productions it's one hundred percent.

Dad secretly wishes he were a writer/director instead of a producer. That's probably why he suggested I use my free time in the office to try scriptwriting. I said I didn't have any ideas for a script. He said, "Write what you know. Look around. Listen in on conversations. Then write a little scene. I wish I'd done that when I was your age. It's a big advantage to start young. You're lucky."

Dad thinks he's doing me this big favor by giving me a job in his office when I'm only thirteen. He promised me that I'd be able to work in the music end of his new film. I was excited about working for Flanders Delmont. He's a composer whose work I really admire. Dad said I would be in Flanders' studio at least half the time. I'd meet other people in the music business. I'd see how Flanders composed and ran his business.

It sounded great until Flanders Delmont decided to run his business out of his home office in Australia.

So here I am, stuck in Schmoozeville with Dad and his new assistant, Duane Richards. Duane is quickly learning the fine art of schmoozing. Today it was, "Maggie, you look so-o-o *very* glamorous today."

What a liar.

I look terrible today. Fat, dull, and so-o-o *very* boring.

DARKNESS

Sunlight ~~summer sun~~ too bright for
the sad day within
Why do troubles haunt
and taunt?
Why do my inner darks ~~cloud out~~ obscure the light?
Are the answers in the darkness?

© Maggie Blume

That is the first poem I've written in weeks. It used to make me feel better to

express my feelings in poetry. But I don't feel any better for writing that poem.
Maybe I should try scriptwriting.

NEVER . . . TELL THE TRUTH
(Inspired by a conversation overheard between Producer and a scriptwriter)

A large office in Hollywood. Producer sits behind a big desk. A writer sits in a small chair facing him.

PRODUCER: We need another chase scene, Ralph. And put a school bus in the car chase scene. Our main character's kid should be on that bus.

WRITER: But Mr. Blume, our main character doesn't have a kid.

PRODUCER: Then we'll give him one. I know you, Ralph. You can work it in. You've done a great job. Let the bus be central in the chase. It can go off one of those cliffs in the Hollywood Hills.

WRITER: *Do you want the kid injured or killed?*

PRODUCER: *Both.*

WRITER: *Both?*

PRODUCER: *We think he's dead, but he's only injured — seriously injured. We don't know if he'll make it. Put in a hospital scene. (He gets up, a signal that it's time for the writer to leave.) Why don't you come by the house for a drink, say around seven? There'll be some people there I'd love you to meet.*

WRITER: *(smiling) Great. Love to.*

Dad is already looking for a *new* writer to rewrite the *Never* script. Everyone on the project knows it. But that night, when the writer came to the house, Dad and his business partners in the film acted like he was the hottest writer in Hollywood. I hate all that phoniness. Hate it.

Dad is back from one of his wheeler-dealer lunches. I better hit the photocopy machine.

Amalia called. There's a Vanish rehearsal tonight. The band hasn't practiced much this summer. We all have summer jobs with different work schedules. Talking to Amalia made me wish we had more time to hang out together. She's such a neat person and a great band manager. Maybe we will hang out, now that Vanish is rehearsing again.

Amalia and Justin are picking me up. I haven't seen Justin in two weeks. I'm so nervous about seeing him again. I can't figure out if he likes me or not. Sometimes we really seem to click. And ten minutes later I think I imagined it.

Justin is going to try out for the band tonight. If he's in the band he'll be at every rehearsal. Then I know I'd see him at least once a week. That would be great. I think.

Amalia told me that Justin has been practicing guitar for hours every day. That he's doing it so he can be in the band. "He's doing it because of YOU," she said.

"He said that?" I asked.

"Not in so many words," Amalia admitted. "But he did say how much he liked EVERYONE who played in the band. Trust me, he likes you."

I wish I could believe her. Justin is everything I would want in a boyfriend — thoughtful, interesting, smart, cute, fun. And he acts like he's *just* Justin. No schmoozing. No phoniness.

But Justin isn't my boyfriend. I'm such a fool. Why would he like me?

I called Mom to tell her about the rehearsal. I could tell she was disappointed I wasn't going to be home for "a nice family dinner." *I* don't think of our family dinners as "nice." Zeke usually talks about some adventure game he plays on the Internet, as if it's real life. Dad complains about all the other sharks in the movie business or tells Zeke and me how we should live our lives.

And we all try to pretend we're not noticing how much Mom is drinking.

My mother drinks too much.

When she drinks too much she has a faraway look in her eyes, like she isn't focusing on me or what I'm saying.

It's strange that I'm writing about this, because Mom has been much better lately.

I just hope she isn't reaching for a drink right now. And if she is, I hope it's not because I won't be home for dinner.

Maybe I should go home instead of to rehearsal?

That's crazy.

If I stopped seeing my friends so Mom wouldn't drink, I could never go out. Besides, it wouldn't stop her.

11:13 P.M.

Dinner: Tossed salad (NO dressing), diet Coke, 3 french fries.

At six o'clock I went into Dad's office and told him about the Vanish rehearsal. I could tell he was disappointed that Vanish hadn't vanished.

He asked me who was taking James's place.

I told him that another guy, Justin, was going to try out. I hope I didn't blush when I said Justin's name. The last thing I need from Dad is an interrogation about Justin.

I hate how Dad wants to produce *my* life.

After work, I waited outside for Justin and Amalia to pick me up. Amalia was sitting in front with Justin, so I hopped in the back.

I hadn't seen Justin in a couple of weeks. He looked as good to me as ever. Wrong. He looked BETTER.

Justin made eye contact with me in the rearview mirror. His brown eyes were smiling — dancing, really. I *love* his eyes.

"It'll be great to hear you sing again, Maggie," he said. "You've given Vanish a new life."

I don't happen to agree with him. But I'm still glad he sort-of-said that he likes my singing.

When we walked into Rico's garage, Patti did a little drumroll to mark our entrance. Bruce strummed something very low on his bass. It felt great to be back.

Justin is now officially in the band. He definitely knows enough guitar to play behind Rico. But my singing was horrid. My voice was weak and raspy. I was embarrassed when I sang "Hey, Down There." Sometimes lyrics are *too* personal.

When I finished, Amalia clapped. "I love that song," she said. I know she was just trying to make me feel better.

But Rico told the truth. "Hey, Maggie," he called to me. "How about writing us a new song?"

"Good idea," agreed Justin.

I knew it. They hated my old song. I'd made a fool of myself. And I looked terrible. If I could lose five pounds maybe I'd look more like a lead singer and less like Ms. Plain Jane.

I couldn't look at Justin for the rest of the rehearsal.

We all went out to a burger joint afterward. I hate those places. They smell greasy and everyone makes a pig of themselves.

I ordered the house salad with dressing on the side. Everyone else ordered the quarter-pounder burger special. I wasn't even tempted. It's disgusting.

"Maggie, I don't believe you're not having a burger," Amalia exclaimed. "You really need to eat something."

Everybody, including the waitress, looked at me.

I reminded Amalia I don't eat red meat.

"Then try their garden burger," suggested Justin. "I've had them. They're good."

I said thanks, but no thanks.

It would be easier to diet if everyone would stop trying to feed me. Why can't they see how fat I am? They say that I'm not, but I AM.

By next week's rehearsal I am going to

lose five pounds. That's the equivalent of 20 quarter-pound burgers. I imagine 20 burgers plastered to my thighs and stomach. Boy, will I be glad to be rid of that fat.

DAISY PETALS

~~He loves me~~
~~He loves me not~~
Our eyes meet ~~but~~
In the rearview mirror.
He holds the gaze.
He loves me.
An hour passes.
Our eyes meet again.
He quickly looks away.
He loves me not.
A dream
A fantasy
~~A mirage~~
No oasis in the desert.
Dry petals in the wind.

© Maggie Blume

That poem will NEVER be a song. No way, no . . .

Zeke came into my room looking very glum. He walked over to my desk and stood beside me. I closed my laptop and my poetry journal and asked him what was up.

"You can make Dad do anything you want," he said. "Tell him I shouldn't be forced to go to tennis camp."

First, I reminded Zeke that I can't make Dad do what I want. No more than he can. Then I asked him why he's so dead set against going to tennis camp.

"I hate tennis," he said. "*I do not want to go to tennis camp.* Do NOT. Not. Please. Please. Puh-lease tell them not to send me."

He threw a glossy pamphlet on my laptop. "This came with the list of stuff I have to bring," he moaned. "They have dances. *And* dance classes. I have to bring a *sport jacket.*"

I opened the brochure. One photo was of four perfectly groomed kids in tennis whites, playing doubles. Another was of a victorious Manor Court Tennis Team holding up a gold trophy. Then I saw the photo that upset Zeke. A smiling boy and girl, arm in arm, gliding across a dance floor.

The idea of Zeke asking some girl to dance is too funny. I had to hold back a smile.

I told him I'd talk to Dad on the way to work tomorrow. But right now, I don't hold out much hope.

I know how Zeke feels. I'm always doing things because Dad thinks they're "good for me."

One of Dad's favorite lines is, "Trust me on this one, Maggie." Another one is, "You'll thank me for this someday."

Like my piano lessons. There are times when I don't want to practice. There was even a period when I wanted to quit. Sometimes the only reason I practice is because I don't want to disappoint Dad.

Now I'm glad that I have a strong musical background. Which means Dad was right.

Why does that bug me so much?

I have to write a new song for Vanish. I don't have any idea what to write. This time I am *not* going to write about myself.

Tuesday 7/14
11:20 A.M.

Breakfast: ¾ cup cereal with skim milk, banana.
My New Motto: Eat to live. Don't live to eat.

Mom came by the office to tell Dad and
me that she's been chosen to be the
chairperson of a fund-raiser for Hollywood
Cares for Animals (HCA). Raising money for
an animal shelter is a good cause. But
putting on a fund-raiser is a big
responsibility. It might be good for Mom. As
long as it's a big success.
Last May, Mom was in charge of a ten-
mile run to raise money for an international
food relief fund. It NEVER rains in Los
Angeles in May, but that day it poured. It was
like throwing a big party and having no one
come. (She sure drank that day. And the day
after. And the day after that.)
I walked with Mom to the elevator. She
said she hoped I'd help her with the benefit
since it's a charity I'm interested in. Which is
true. I'm amazed at how many stray animals

end up in our neighborhood. I don't understand how anyone could abandon an animal.

It's turning into a busy summer. I have my job, Vanish rehearsals, and Mom's benefit for HCA.

Good.

I won't have time to think about food.

Or Justin.

Does he think about me?

I doubt it.

Why should he?

8:35 P.M.

Lunch: 1 container low-fat yogurt, 1 apple (small), 1 chocolate chip cookie (I have NO SELF-CONTROL).
Dinner (at home): Salad (no dressing), baked potato (no butter or sour cream),
½ portion of baked fish, 3 bites of fruit pie.

Eating at home drives me crazy.

"Don't you want sour cream for your potato?" asks Dad.

"Darling, you have to finish your dessert," says Mom.

"Are you on a diet, Fatty?" asks Zeke.

"She is *not* fat — she's too thin!" groans Dad. (Yeah, right.)

I said I was full and gave the rest of my pie to Zeke.

I like Pilar. And I like her cooking. Which probably is the reason I'm such a tub-a-lub. Pilar is always making cookies for Zeke and me, homemade breads to go with dinner, and the most fattening main courses imaginable.

This is *not* the best situation for someone with very little self-control who is trying to lose weight.

When Zeke heard about the benefit for HCA he said he'd pass on going to camp so he could help. Zeke hates benefits, which should have proven to our parents how much he doesn't want to go to this camp.

Mom told him how much fun she had at summer camp when she was eleven years old.

Dad said, "Now, son, let's not go on about

the camp thing. You're going. You'll thank me someday."

Poor Zeke.

Mom seemed okay at dinner — only one glass of wine. She's practicing more self-control than I am. But I can tell she's already nervous about the HCA benefit. The person who was in charge had to quit because of a family problem, so things that should have been done by now were neglected. The dinner and auction are only two weeks away and Mom found out that the invitations just went out a week or so ago. They also need more items to auction off. Mom has loads of ideas, like dinner for four, prepared by some famous chef at your house, or a week at some celebrity's great beach house. But Mom has to convince a famous chef to make the dinner for free and a famous person to let strangers stay in his or her great beach house for a week. She needs at least fifteen more items like that for the auction.

I promised to help Mom on Saturday.

I'm glad I have my own phone line. Mom

is going to be on the house line nonstop until the benefit.

But really — why did I say that about the phone?

What difference does it make?

No one is trying to call me.

Certainly not Justin.

Wednesday 7/15
2:04 P.M.

Breakfast: ½ grapefruit, piece of toast with jam (no butter).
Lunch: 1 scoop tuna (no mayo), 4 celery sticks, 4 potato chips (4 too many).

I can't believe it. Justin called me. He was so sweet. First he apologized for calling me at work. I said it wasn't a problem. He said there's a rehearsal tomorrow night if I can come. I said yes and he said great.

I couldn't think of anything else to say, but I didn't want to say good-bye. I heard a dog barking in the background and asked him if he has a dog.

"That's Jazz," he said. "Come here, Jazz. Say hello to Maggie."

Jazz barked into the phone.

"Jazz is a mutt," Justin told me. "I picked him out in an HCA shelter when I was in the second grade. He's a terrific dog."

I couldn't believe it. Not only is Justin cute, nice, and musical. He also has a sweet dog he adopted from a shelter!

I told Justin about Curtis, our kitten. Then I babbled on about Mom's fund-raiser for HCA. Finally I said, "I guess I better get back to work."

"Want a ride to the rehearsal tomorrow night?" he asked.

I looked down at my work calendar and read. "Thursday. 3:00 P.M. Auditions for *Never*. Go with Dad." I didn't know where the auditions were being held.

"I don't know where I'll be before rehearsal," I told Justin. Boy, did that sound stupid.

"Okay," he said. "See you there, then. 'Bye."

And he hung up.

I can't believe I acted so dumb. I didn't even thank him for offering me a ride. And now that I think about it, it doesn't mean anything special that he called me. Amalia probably asked him to.

Thursday 7/16
2:30 P.M.

Breakfast: Low-fat cereal with skim milk.
Lunch: Orange, 2 chocolate chip cookies (low fat).
Note: I have only lost one pound so far. *I WILL NOT EAT SO MUCH.*

Too busy to write. Going to *Never* audition, then band rehearsal.

Snack: 9 potato chips.
Supper: 1 slice pizza with cheese scraped off, diet soda.

I shouldn't have eaten those potato chips. I have NO self-control. I'm sure that the actress Dad chose as the lead for *Never* wouldn't be caught dead eating potato chips. She has a perfect figure, not an ounce of fat. She used to be a model.

Why do I always think I'm hungry? I say over and over to myself: I am not hungry. I will stick to my diet. I am not hungry. I will stick to my diet.

Why do they have to call it die-it? That makes dieting sound awful and negative. Why not call it live-it? That's it. I'm on a live-it. Eat to live. Tomorrow I'll have tuna for lunch — no bread.

I'm thinking about food again. Think about something else.

Justin.

Why am I obsessed with him?

Because he is cute and kind and smart and talented, that's why.

And he has a dog named Jazz.

Dad's new chauffeur, Reg, gave me a ride to the rehearsal. Even though I was twenty minutes late, I got out two blocks from Rico's. I didn't want anyone to see me arrive in a limo!

I heard the band practicing from half a block away. It sounded great.

I wonder: Am I good enough to be singing with them?

What if they play better and better and I don't improve as a singer?

Amalia was standing inside the door. She gave me a big hug. Rico, Patti, and Bruce waved to me. Justin didn't.

"We're all going out for pizza after," said Amalia. "Can you?"

I told her yes, as long as I was home by ten-thirty. I asked in a whisper if she had asked Justin to call me. She said he'd offered to make calls for her because she can't make calls from her job at the ice-cream shop. I asked her if he offered to call *everyone*. "Everyone else already knew," she answered.

I still don't know if Justin called me because he wanted to, or to help out Amalia.

As I headed for the band, Justin looked up. His face broke into a huge grin. "Hi," he called out. "You got here."

"Yes, here I am," I said.

What a dumb thing to say.

I sucked in my big stomach and went over to the mike.

We ran through "Fallen Angel" five times so Justin could learn it. It was hard to concentrate on the lyrics. My stomach was rumbling and I had a headache, probably from worrying about being at rehearsal on time.

I tried to put my mind and heart into my lyrics. I was thinking about Justin when I sang the last lines, "Won't you come with me? / 'Cause I don't want to be / A fallen angel / A fallen angel."

We rehearsed some more numbers. Everyone had an upbeat attitude. Rico's parents brought in some sodas and snacks for us. We stood around drinking and eating (only a diet Coke for me). Everyone talked about how good the band was sounding and where they thought we could improve. Justin was standing near me. Very near.

"Working on a new song?" he asked.

"Not yet," I said. "How about you? Are you going to compose for the band?"

"I'm not in that league yet," he answered.

Justin put his hand on my arm. It was like he was hugging me. That's how it made me feel. "You coming out with us after?" he asked.

All I could think was, *Please don't take your hand off my arm.* I managed to nod.

"Good," he said. Then he went back to his guitar.

After rehearsal we walked to a pizza place near Rico's. Justin and Patti paired off. I wondered if Patti was sick of Bruce and was making a play for Justin. Or was Justin making a play for her? Whichever way it worked . . . they were laughing and talking up a storm. I hated that they were having such a good time together. The jealousy must have shown because Amalia pulled me aside to say that Patti asked Justin to walk with her.

Whatever.

All I know is that *I've* never made him laugh like that.

Why do people always have to EAT when they hang out together? I tried to act lively and be part of the crowd at the pizza parlor. But it was hard to be jolly when everyone else was wolfing down slice after slice of pizza and nagging me to join in.

"Don't take off the cheese, that's the best part."

"Have another slice, Maggie."

"I can't believe you're only eating one slice."

They just don't get it.

Justin asked me about my job. Everyone listened when I described the plot of *Never*. I made fun of my dad's film. I felt disloyal, but I didn't want them to think I liked that junk.

On the way back to Rico's, Justin walked next to me. I figured he only did it because

Patti went off in the other direction with Bruce.

I asked him questions about his dog. I told him how I wanted to be a vet. He said he assumed I wanted to be a professional singer. Ha!

Does he really think I'm that good?

No, he couldn't. Because I'm not.

He just thinks that I *think* I'm that good. How awful.

When we were almost at Rico's house, I realized that I hadn't asked Justin if he could give me a ride home. I had just assumed he would. But what if he hadn't assumed what I assumed? I blurted out something about needing a ride.

He grinned and said, "Isn't the limo from your dad's company picking you up?" I could tell he was joking, but it hurt. Maybe that's why he thinks I think I could be a professional singer. Because my dad is a big deal in the entertainment industry. It was an awful moment. I didn't say anything. Finally, Justin broke the silence by saying of course he'd give me a ride home. He was giving

Amalia a ride. Besides, my house was on his way.

Amalia jumped into the backseat of the car. I realized that if I got in the back with her, Justin would be left alone in front — just like in a chauffeured car. I got in the front.

When I put on the seat belt it made an indent across my fat belly. It was a good reminder of WHY I take the cheese off my pizza. I put my backpack on my lap.

Amalia and Justin started talking about a festival of rock concert films that's playing in Anaheim. Justin suggested that we all go on July 25th, when they're showing *Rockers Roll.* He thinks I sing like Maxie Benox. (I'll never be that good.)

I've already seen the film. My dad knows the producers, so we went to a private screening. But I didn't tell Amalia and Justin that. I wanted to go with them.

"Next Saturday I can't, Justin," Amalia said. "I'm going to a baby shower for my cousin."

Justin turned to me and asked if I could go anyway.

I couldn't believe it. Justin was asking me on a date. Sort of.

"Yes," I blurted out. "I mean, I think so. I just have to check with my parents."

Lame, lame, lame.

"Okay," he said. "I'll pick up tickets."

To do:
- Ask Mom and Dad for permission to go out with Justin Saturday night.
- Lose three pounds by Saturday.

11:06 P.M.

Amalia called to talk about my date with Justin. I asked her if she thought it was a real "date." Then an idea struck me like lightning. Justin was probably going to ask Rico, Bruce, and Patti too.

"Maybe he will," Amalia said. "Maybe he did. But I know that they can't go. Everyone else is busy. It's you and Justin — alone."

"Yess!" I shouted.

Then reality hit me.

"What am I going to wear, Amalia?" I moaned into the receiver. "What will we talk about? Help! I'm so nervous."

Amalia was great. She calmed me right down. She's going to help me figure out what to wear. And we're even going to think about subjects I can bring up to talk about. Maybe I'll make a list.

I'll lose at least three pounds by Saturday. I will.

I hope Justin isn't too disappointed that I'm the only one who's available to go to the film.

Saturday 7/18
6:24 P.M.

Weight: 100! Not perfect, but getting there.

I'm not going to write down what I eat anymore. It makes food too important in my life. I just won't eat.

Started the day by attending a meeting Mom had at our house for her committee.

Good news: Mom didn't serve her famous Bloody Marys, and, as far as I can tell, she didn't sneak drinks.

Curtis attended, and some of the committee members fed him nibbles of smoked salmon. We've decided he's the mascot of the fund-raiser.

While Mom conducted the meeting, her committee and I started stuffing donation requests into envelopes and putting on address labels and postage stamps. We used stamps with pictures of cats and dogs. Mom's idea. I thought that was a nice touch.

Our goal was to get fifteen hundred envelopes ready and at the post office before it closed at one o'clock. Mom asked me to bring the mailings to the post office and see them safely on their way. There are times when I have to admit that it's handy to have a car and driver.

Just before I left for the post office, one of the HCA shelters called to say they didn't have mailings for their employees and volunteers to send out. Mom asked me to swing by there too.

She gave me a big hug and my hair a little tug, the way she used to when I was a kid. "Thank you, honey," she said. "I couldn't do this without you."

It's been a long time since she hugged me like that. It was just like the old Mom I can only vaguely remember.

I had never been to an HCA shelter. This one was in a concrete building in a run-down neighborhood. I think it used to be a garage. There was a sign on the front that read ANIMAL RESCUE.

I went inside. An elderly man was manning the front desk. He wore a name tag that read VOLUNTEER. A woman in a pale blue lab coat was giving him directions on what to do if someone called reporting a stray cat or dog. She was very efficient and seemed a little stressed out.

Finally, the man looked up and asked if he could help me.

"I'm Maggie Blume," I told him. I put the pack of mailings on the desk. "My mother asked me to drop these off. Someone called and asked for them."

The woman smiled at me. "That was me," she said. "I'm Piper Klein." She shook my hand and told me how lucky HCA was that Mom was willing to take over the chairperson's job for the benefit. I told her how much I admired the work of the HCA shelters and how a friend of mine had gotten his dog from one of them.

"Have you been here before?" she asked.

I told her I hadn't and she asked me if I'd like a tour.

I followed her into the back.

A chorus of barks greeted us. "We have a dog run out back," Piper explained. "But they have to take turns. Most of the day they're here."

I counted twelve dogs. Mutts, pedigrees, short-hair, long-hair, small, big. There was one collie whose eyes broke my heart. He pushed his nose through the bars of his crate and whimpered. It was as if he were saying, "Take me. Love me."

Piper saw me looking at him. "Isn't he beautiful?" she said. "That's Laddie. He's been here three months. Our problem is that we have more people bringing us animals then we have taking them home." She went on to say that one of the things HCA wants to do with the money Mom raises is to have an advertising campaign. "A lot of people don't even know we exist," she told me.

I looked around at the other dogs. Each was cuter than the next.

"We should have photos of these dogs at the fund-raiser," I said. "Cats too. Big poster-sized photos. People will see where their money is going. And maybe some of them will decide to adopt."

"That's a wonderful idea," Piper said. She studied me for a second. "You really like animals, don't you?"

"I might be a veterinarian," I told her.

"Good for you."

She showed me the cat room next. The cats were as wonderful as the dogs and just as heartbreaking. All those animals living in crates. I wondered what kind of life Curtis would have had if I hadn't kept him. Would he have ended up in a shelter? Would anyone have adopted him?

Piper has a cramped office at the end of the hall. The window overlooks the dog run. "I have my office back here so I can keep an eye on things," she said. Her desk was piled with papers. "My intern quit yesterday. She thought this would be a good summer job for meeting cute guys and all she met were cute dogs and cats." She smiled at me. "I wish I could have an intern like you. But you're probably all booked up for the summer."

I told her I was working for my father.

She was disappointed. She's placed an ad in tomorrow's paper. She said she hoped someone as enthusiastic as me would see it and call her.

Basically, Piper needs me. Dad doesn't.

I can't get those animals out of my mind. I'd rather help them than work in Schmoozeville.

Why can't I do what I want?

It's not fair.

I wish I had the courage to quit my job with Dad.

If only I could get Mom on my side.

I feel awful. Like I've done something wrong.

Guilty as accused.

But what crime have I committed?

Tonight we had a "nice" five-course family dinner because it was Zeke's last night before camp. Dad made a toast to Zeke and said he was sure Zeke would have a great time at tennis camp. Zeke mumbled he was sure he wouldn't.

Pilar came around with the soup course. I told her that I would skip it.

She frowned.

Dad launched into his Why-This-Camp-Is-Good-for-You-Son speech for the umpteenth time.

Mom took a gulp of wine.

We were off to a bad start.

During the salad course Mom told Dad what she was doing for the fund-raiser. She said she was having trouble finding people willing to donate things to be auctioned off.

Apparently, there's another big benefit in Hollywood the same night. She told Dad she's worried everyone will go to that benefit instead of hers.

Then she refilled her wine glass.

Pilar served cheese tortellini in a white cream sauce. I told her I didn't want any.

Dad noticed and frowned.

Pilar glared at me.

I hate eating with my family.

No one said anything for a few minutes. Then Dad grumbled about problems he's having with the casting of *Never*.

Next Pilar served the main course — steak. I gave Zeke my steak after Pilar left the dining room.

"How was your day, Maggie?" Dad asked.

I told him about the shelter. Then I blurted out, "They need an intern for the rest of the summer. Piper — she's the one in charge — asked me if I'd like to have the job. It's a worthy cause."

"It certainly is," said Mom.

"You already have a job this summer," Dad reminded me.

"But it's not the job I want," I replied. Then — without taking a breath so he couldn't interrupt me — I reminded him that I wasn't working with the composer the way he'd promised and that he didn't really need me.

"It would be good for the benefit if my daughter works at an HCA shelter," Mom said. She tapped her wine glass. Sometimes she's nervous around Dad. Especially if she's contradicting him.

Pilar served dessert — ice cream and hot fudge. I knew that Zeke would polish mine off for me. So I let Pilar put a serving at my place.

When she left the room, Dad pointed his spoon at me. "Are you telling me you would back out of your commitment to me because you found something that you like better?"

"Well, you made a commitment too, Dad," I said in a wavering voice.

Do not cry, I warned myself. *Do not cry.*

I sat straighter and tried to look my father in the eye.

I couldn't.

But I kept talking. "You said I'd be working with Flanders, but instead all I'm doing is pouring coffee and running the photocopy machine. You have plenty of people who could do those things. Piper doesn't have anyone. Those dogs and cats need me. You don't."

"I certainly don't need someone with an attitude like that!" Dad replied. "And don't you raise your voice to me."

"You're the one who's screaming," I mumbled.

He glared at me again and took a deep breath. "This summer is stressful for me already, Maggie," he said in an even voice. "The last thing I need is to baby-sit for a grumpy teenager. So go ahead and quit." He leaned forward and lowered his voice almost to a whisper. "Just know this: You've disappointed me."

End of speech.

End of meal.

WHOSE LIFE IS THIS?

Whose life is this?
Don't you know
That I am not yours to mold
Like clay
I am
Not your dream child
Not your wish come true
How can I find my own way
If you always tell me what to do?

© Maggie Blume

Midnight

At eleven o'clock someone knocked on my bedroom door and asked, "Are you okay, Maggie?"

It wasn't my mother, who was probably having a stiff drink because I ruined dinner.

And it wasn't my father, who was probably waiting for me to apologize and beg for my job back at Blume Productions.

It was Zeke.

"I'm okay," I called. "Come on in."

I told him I hate it when Dad tries to control every move I make.

"I know what you mean," Zeke said. He was carrying a turtle in each hand. "Will you take care of Zeus and Jupiter while I'm gone?" he asked as he laid them on my desk.

I held Zeus in the palm of my hand. His shell reached all the way to my fingertips. I stroked his shell and his head pulled out and snaked up to me. I told Zeke I'd be glad to take care of his turtles. He said he had e-mailed me directions for their care. "So you have to check your e-mail," he said.

Zeke loves to go online and exchange e-mail with his friends. I don't have anyone to e-mail, except Zeke. Whenever I check my e-mail, all I have are silly messages from my brother.

We moved Zeus and Jupiter's box into my room. Curtis was thrilled. Whenever the turtles are around he thinks it's his job to watch them.

I told Zeke I was sorry that he had to go to camp. I added that he was probably better off there than at our house. It would be a lot more peaceful.

"I'd rather be here," he said. "I don't want to miss anything."

"You mean, like another fight between me and Dad? Is that your idea of entertainment?"

"Who's going to be on your side if I'm not here?" he asked.

That was so sweet. I couldn't believe it. Sometimes my brother surprises me.

He asked me if I wanted to see how he plays his Internet adventure game. I agreed, and he went back to his room for his laptop. We hooked it up to my phone line and sat together at my desk. Zeke said that no matter what, he was going to find time to go online at camp "between tennis lessons and dancing lessons." I said that they probably had phone lines all over that camp. "You should call me while you're at camp," I added.

He said he would, and I had to promise to tell him EVERYTHING that was happening at home. Even unhappy stuff. I think he meant about Mom's drinking. I'm not really sure how much Zeke understands about that problem. I don't know much about it myself, since no one ever talks about it.

After Zeke turned off his computer he went to the kitchen and brought back a brownie and milk for himself and a diet soda for me. While he ate I told him more about the animal shelter and that I hoped Piper hadn't already filled the position.

Zeke took a bite of his brownie.

"Hey, this is like one of those sleepover parties you have with your friends," he said. "Does that mean I can sleep here?"

"Sure," I said. "The extra bed is made up."

I'm glad he's sleeping in my room tonight. I guess I'll try to sleep now too.

Zeke made me feel better.

I am going to miss him. A lot.

Lost another pound.

I must keep telling myself: I am not hungry.

I am not hungry.

I am not hungry.

What if Piper hired someone else to work in the shelter?

I left her phone messages at home and at the shelter this afternoon. I wonder how many people answered the ad in the paper. I'm not the only teenager in Palo City who loves animals and would love that job.

Why didn't I think to call her at home last night?

I'm such a jerk.

Zeke is at camp. I hope he isn't totally miserable.

Mom and Dad are at a dinner party. I hope Mom doesn't drink too much.

I keep thinking about the fight I had with Dad last night and how I've disappointed him. Whenever I remember our fight I feel like

I'm crying inside. I wish I could talk to someone about it.

I would never tell Justin. He might think I'm a complaining spoiled rich brat. He'd probably be right.

Maybe I could talk to Amalia. No. It took her a long time to find a summer job, so she'd think I was ungrateful to quit a good job.

Some things you have to keep to yourself.

7:23 P.M.

Piper just called. She's hiring me! I start tomorrow.

She said she hopes I'm not afraid of hard work. I'm not! It'll be easier to lose weight if I'm really busy.

I'm going to e-mail Zeke right away and tell him the good news.

Skipped lunch.

Supper: Salad, small can of tuna, ¼ bagel (no butter), apple.

I love my new job.

It is so wonderful to do something IMPORTANT.

Job Description: Feed dogs and cats. Organize and supervise dog run. Answer phone during breaks and lunch hour.

Piper says with more money they could redo the back of the building so every dog has its own run. She has loads of great ideas for improving the shelter.

I wore new chinos and a white T-shirt to work today. Piper said I was dressed way too fancy for working at the shelter. "Save your good pants and T-shirts. On this job we don't care how you look. We care about what you do."

Dad was always commenting on what I wore to his office. One day he'd say, "Isn't that a little preppy?" The next day it would be, "That's too dressy for the office."

How can a person have so many clothes and not know what to wear? I don't have any style. Thank goodness Amalia is helping me pick out something to wear for my date with Justin.

Meanwhile, the police brought an injured dog to the shelter. She was hit by a car on the freeway. She's a standard-poodle mix, but she didn't have a collar. We named her Roxie.

Besides a broken leg, Roxie is undernourished and big patches of her fur are missing. Piper said she was pretty sure that Roxie once had owners but has probably been a stray for months. The vet set her leg and prescribed a special extra-nourishing diet. Piper said that the collie I like so much, Laddie, looked that bad when he came in. Now Laddie looks great.

Laddie would be a good model for one of the posters for the benefit.

To do: Talk to Mom about finding a photographer to take pics of animals at shelter.

THROWN-AWAY PET

Thrown-away pet
~~wandering on.~~
Crossing the highway.
Horns honk.
Cars swerve.
Fear.
Abandoned. Alone. ~~And you left all alone~~
Are men's hearts made of stone?

Thrown-away pet.
Running for safety.
Car hits.
Bones break.
Pain.

Abandoned. Alone.
Are men's hearts made of stone?

© Maggie Blume

Maybe those could be the lyrics of a song someday.

Maybe. It would make kind of a tragic song, though.

Mom and Dad both had dinner dates and it's Pilar's day off. Good. There's no one here to bug me about eating. I'd rather eat alone anyway.

But this house is SO big when you're the only one in it. It can be creepy.

11:09 P.M.

I heard Mom come in a little while ago. I met her in the family room. She was pouring herself a vodka and tonic (heavy on the vodka, light on the tonic). As I passed our crystal angel statue I touched her wing. I always do that for good luck. The statue is of 2 figures — an angel protecting a child. I love that the angel's wings are as big as the child and that the child looks up at the angel with total trust. The statue has been in the family room for as long as I can remember.

I took a live-it soda from the refrigerator under the bar and sat on a stool next to Mom.

"Well, that was the most boring meeting I have ever been to," she mumbled.

"What meeting?" I asked.

"With my so-called committee. We ate at the Tafts Hotel and tried out the meal they planned for the benefit. Boring food. Boring people. Really, I don't know why I'm bothering with this auction."

She had that faraway, unfocused look in her eyes. A knot of fear formed in my stomach. How can she put on the benefit if she starts drinking?

I reminded her that she accepted the chairperson's job because HCA is an important cause. I started to tell her about the dog they brought in today, but she interrupted me.

"Maggie, we have to do something with your hair. Before the benefit." She looked at me as if I disgusted her. "And let's give a little thought to what you're wearing. Not that I have time." She sighed and took another slug of her drink.

"Did you complain to the people at the hotel about the menu for the banquet?" I asked.

"Why bother? Besides, most people don't care about the food as long as we serve a salad. Everyone in Hollywood is on a diet."

"Did you find more things to auction off?" I asked.

"Not enough. They can't call me in to be chairperson at the last minute and expect me to perform miracles."

I wanted to get away from Mom. I hate her attitude when she's drinking. But I was worried that the auction would be a failure. Then what would happen to the shelter?

"Did you tell your committee about the animal photo idea?" I asked.

"What photo idea?"

The knot in my stomach was tightening. I reminded her about my idea to have big photos of animals from the shelter posted at the benefit.

"Oh, that," she said. "It can be your project. I don't have time." She went behind the bar and poured herself another drink.

Mom is falling into her usual trap. I know she's drinking because she's afraid the benefit will be a failure. But if she's drinking instead of working on the benefit it *will* be a failure. What a mess.

Drunk or not, Mom was right about one thing. I LOOK AWFUL. I just tried on about a thousand outfits and I look terrible in all of them.

FAT. *FAT.* FAT.

Buying new clothes isn't the answer. Losing weight is.

I've changed my goal. I'm going to lose *five* pounds by Saturday. I just won't eat. My body can eat its own fat.

I want to look like the actress Dad hired for his film. She'd look gorgeous in any of my clothes.

I hate my stomach. Five pounds won't be enough. But it's a start.

Tuesday 7/21

12:34 P.M.

Skipping lunch. At front desk while volunteer goes to lunch.

Piper was right about this job being hard

work. I didn't stop for five seconds all morning.

I talked to her about the animal photographs for the benefit. We decided we need a really good photographer if the blowups are going to look good. Piper said she doesn't know any professional photographers. I said I'd ask my dad to give me names of people and I'd call them.

I was embarrassed that I asked Piper for help in the first place. She shouldn't have to worry about the benefit. Called Dad, but he's not at his office.

E-mail from Zeke:

Margaret Blume. Help! I am captive in outer space. Aliens in white shorts carrying strange weapons hit yellow balls ☹ ☹ ☹ at me *all day long*. No fun. Dance lesson tonight. Save me. H-e-l-l-l-l-p-p-p-p! Beg the superior powers to send rescue troops to free me. Please.

Poor Zeke.

A woman just called the shelter. She found a litter of abandoned kittens near a supermarket. She's bringing them in. Have to go prepare a crate for them.

Lost 1 pound, 4 to go.

Busy, busy at work. The kittens are so cute. Five gray-and-white fluff balls. But they were taken from their mother too soon. The smallest one has to be bottle-fed. We named him Little Guy. Don't know if he'll make it.

Dad in. Mom out.

Mom left a note: *Went shopping for dress for the stupid benefit. Home for dinner.*

She wasn't home for dinner. She must have stopped for a drink . . . or two . . . or three on the way home. When things get bad, she likes to do that.

Pilar made dinner. Roasted chicken, mashed potatoes, string beans, and salad. I skipped lunch and only ate *a little* supper. Dad kept nagging me to eat more.

I don't understand my parents. They want me to look perfect. And then they try to keep me fat.

Mom's phone line rang five times during dinner. I answered it in case they were calls about the benefit. It was also a way to escape Pilar's food.

All the messages were people calling back about things they were asked to donate for the auction. Mom had left them messages to call her after seven when she'd be home — which she wasn't.

I acted like I was Mom's assistant and thanked them for returning her call. Between phone calls I found the list of people she'd called and what she wanted them to volunteer. I convinced the next caller — the owner of a fancy bakery — to donate pastries for a dessert party for thirty people.

When I went back to the table, I told Dad about my idea for big pictures of shelter animals at the benefit and asked him if he knew a photographer who might take pictures for free. He said he'd make a few calls after dinner. "It might help your mother," he concluded.

I could tell he was discouraged about Mom, but he didn't say anything more to me about her.

Next, I told him about the e-mail from Zeke. "He's *not* coming home," Dad said. He looked at me over the rim of his coffee cup and raised an eyebrow. "I'm not raising my kids to be quitters."

What he meant was, *"Quitters like you."*

I decided it wasn't the best time to remind Dad that I won't be home tomorrow night. That I have a Vanish rehearsal.

11:30 P.M.

Mom just came in. I can hear her and Dad arguing in the living room. I'm not going to go downstairs. I'll go over her messages with her in the morning. I hope she's not too hungover to deal with it.

Rehearsal was terrible. I mean, *I* was terrible. Everyone else played great, but my voice sounded weak and lifeless.

During the break, Rico took me aside and asked me to put more energy into my singing.

After Rico talked to me, Amalia came over. "Are you okay?" she asked.

"Sure," I answered. "I know I'm not singing well tonight. The band is getting better and better. I'm not. I'm the opposite."

"You're just having an off night," Amalia said. "You don't seem to be concentrating on the lyrics."

"I know."

I didn't tell her that if I concentrated on some of the lyrics, like the ones for "Fallen Angel," I would burst into tears.

Amalia took the diet soda out of my hand and handed me one of the big chocolate chip cookies she'd made for the rehearsal. "Eat this," she ordered. "And have a glass of milk."

I put the cookie down. "I don't like sweets," I told her.

"What *do* you like to eat?" Amalia asked. "I never see you eating. The rest of us stuff our faces and you nibble on practically nothing. Maybe you don't eat enough. You look awfully thin."

"Me, thin?" I said. "That's a joke." I didn't like the way I sounded when I said that. But Amalia irritated me.

Why can't everyone just leave me alone?

"Let's put in another hour," called Rico. "And you're all invited to stay for dinner. Mom and I made Spanish rice, black beans, and fried bananas."

Everyone cheered.

Everyone except me.

"His mother is the best cook," Amalia whispered. "And Rico takes after her. This will be a feast!"

"I have to go home right after rehearsal," I lied.

Amalia asked how I would get home.

"My dad or someone will pick me up," I told her. "It's not a problem."

I was *really* annoyed with Amalia now. MIND YOUR OWN BUSINESS, is what I wanted to say.

I didn't sing any better after the break.

I couldn't concentrate on the lyrics. Too many thoughts and questions were going through my head.

Will Little Guy live?

Will the two photographers I called today call back? Will we have the posters made in time for the benefit?

Is Zeke horribly homesick? I better send him an e-mail tonight.

Is my mother out drinking? I should have stayed home tonight and helped her with the auction.

Is Dad still angry with me for quitting my job? I have to make up with him.

Can I ever be good enough to please my father?

Why hadn't Justin talked to me tonight? Is he sorry he asked me on a "date"?

What can I wear for our so-called date so I don't look like a big, fat slob?

Justin finally talked to me after rehearsal.

"Are you okay?" he asked.

"I was having an off night," I told him. "I'm sorry."

"I wasn't talking about your singing," he said. "You look pale." He touched my cheek with his fingertips. "And you have big circles under your eyes."

I told him I've been working hard and that I was going home early to help my mother with the benefit.

"You're not staying for the Spanish rice?!" he exclaimed.

What is it with everybody and food? Not everyone likes rich, greasy Spanish rice.

"No," I said. "I can't."

I went into Rico's house to phone home for a ride. Mom answered the phone. Reg was picking up Dad, but she said she'd come pick me up. She didn't sound drunk.

Something was going right.

It's a good thing I came home. I got Mom to do a little work on the auction. And both photographers called me back. One really loves animals and has a cat from one of the shelters. She said she'd come by the shelter tomorrow.

Midnight

Amalia called this evening to see how I was feeling, as if I were sick. I told her I was fine, that I just had a lot on my mind. "Like what?" she asked.

I told her about the benefit and added, "I'm worried about my date with Justin."

She's going shopping with me at the mall after work tomorrow. I'll have my hair done at Hair Today, shop for an outfit, and buy some undereye cover makeup.

As soon as Amalia and I hung up, Justin called. I figured he called to break the date. But he only wondered if I was okay.

I told him I was fine.

Then he reminded me about our date. As

if I needed a reminder. He told me he'd pick me up at seven o'clock.

He actually called it a "date." I'm more nervous than ever.

I lost another pound. Two to go.

Thursday 7/23
9:16 A.M.

Little Guy died early this morning.
We're sad at the shelter today.

10:45 P.M.

Zeke phoned me. He went on and on about how much he hates tennis camp. I just listened.

Then he asked me about Mom and Dad.

I told him they were fine.

"Tell me everything," he said. "What's everybody doing?"

I told him a couple of things about the

benefit. But I didn't feel like talking to Zeke. Or anyone else.

I'm just so tired.

Zeke wouldn't give up. "What are they doing now?" he asked.

"Why don't you ask them yourself?" I asked. "They're both here. Call back on the house phone."

"I can't do that!" Zeke shrieked. "I'll say I want to come home and Dad will yell at me for being a quitter."

I'd like to help my brother, but what can I do?

I told him I was exhausted and had to get off the phone.

Everyone is getting on my nerves today.

After work I met Amalia at Hair Today. I couldn't decide how I wanted Darlene to cut my hair. Finally, I followed her suggestion to have it short in the back, slanting to longer in the front. Amalia says it looks great and very "in." I think it makes my face look rounder than ever, meaning fat, which it is.

As we were leaving Hair Today we spotted Sunny and Ducky coming out of a lingerie shop.

I hadn't seen either of them in ages.

"Cool haircut," was Sunny's first comment.

"Way cool," added Ducky.

When I said I wasn't sure I liked it, Sunny suggested I add a colored streak to one side. (But I used to put colors in my hair all the time. I'm a little sick of colored streaks — on me anyway.)

Ducky said that wasn't my style. That everyone has to go with his or her own style.

Right. If you have a style. Which I don't.

Sunny studied me. "Hey, did you lose weight or something?" she asked. "You look good."

At last someone noticed!

"Maybe a little," I said.

"You look like you've lost a lot of weight," said Ducky. "Are you sure you're eating enough?"

"Of course I'm eating enough." I almost added, "That's my problem," but I didn't want to get into a whole discussion about food.

Sunny is model-thin. I wondered if she's dieting too. Or is she one of the lucky ones who doesn't have to worry about what she eats?

I checked Sunny over to see if she'd done any more body piercing. Her ears were studded with a bunch of earrings, which wasn't new. She was still wearing a naval ring. But she'd added something else on her stomach. A small rose tattoo with thorns and leaves curved like a half-moon around the ring. Maybe it's one of those temporary tattoos.

I hope so.

Amalia asked Sunny and Ducky what they were doing at the mall.

Sunny held up a bag. "My mom asked me to get her a new nightgown and a scarf for her head." Then she threw an arm around Ducky's shoulder and said, "Dad let Ducky and me out of Bookstore Jail to run this mission of mercy." She looked around and said sarcastically, "Aren't malls the most exciting places in the world? Almost as much fun as bookstores." She added under her breath, "And hospitals."

"Do you get the idea Sunny doesn't like her job?" Ducky asked.

I wanted to ask Sunny how her mother was doing but decided to wait and ask Ducky when she was out of earshot. (Ducky told me Mrs. Winslow isn't getting any better. I ache for Sunny.)

Ducky said they were on their way to Mario's. That it was All-the-Spaghetti-You-Can-Eat night. He asked me and Amalia to come with them.

"Sure," said Amalia. She turned to me and added, "Is that okay with you?"

Food. Again!

"I'm here to shop," I said. "Not to eat."

"Maggie has a hot date Saturday night," Amalia blurted out.

I elbowed her, but it was too late. Sunny and Ducky were already quizzing me.

After they had the scoop about me, Justin, and the film, Sunny said, "We'll help you pick out something to wear, Maggie." She looked me up and down. I had come right from work so I was wearing dirty jeans and a red T-shirt with the HCA logo. I was dressed like a jerk and I felt like a jerk. I had thought of bringing something to work to change into before I went to the mall. But I couldn't decide what it should be.

I may not like the way Sunny dresses, but at least she has a style. I'm a mishmash of styles, which means *No Style*.

Sunny said I should go to the secondhand store and buy something retro.

Pass.

We went into a boutique.

Ducky wanted me to buy tight, slim pants, a glittery T-shirt, and foxy high heels.

Pass.

Amalia held up a long, flowing skirt and said I should wear it with a string of beads she'd lend me. I didn't even bother to try it on. I knew it would make me look like a balloon.

I picked up a short brown skirt and a

velveteen black top with thin black vertical stripes. I figured dark colors and vertical stripes would make me look thinner.

I put the outfit on and studied myself in the three-way mirror.

I thought the skirt was snug. Amalia, sounding a little doubtful, said that if I really thought it was snug, I should try the next size up (a size four!) and that she'd get it.

I told her not to bother. I sucked in my stomach and silently vowed that it would fit by Saturday.

I ate a salad while they gorged themselves on spaghetti.

Amalia pointed an enormous forkful of spaghetti at me. "This is so good, Maggie," she said. "You have to taste it."

"No, I don't," I shot back. "Leave me alone."

She looked hurt, but I don't care.

Maybe now she'll stop trying to feed me.

I'm exhausted.

I'm going to sleep.

Goal: Forget about food. Don't eat.

Called in sick. Staying home from work today.

Nervous about date.

Nervous about Mom and benefit.

Nervous about date.

Nervous about writing new song for Vanish.

Nervous about date.

Tried on skirt. It almost fits.

2:30 P.M.

Why can't Pilar mind her own business?

Mom and I were working on the benefit in her study. Pilar came in to see what we wanted for lunch. Mom said she'd have an omelette. I said I didn't want anything, that I wasn't hungry.

"That's not healthy," Pilar said. "You're a growing girl! You have to eat."

"I don't want anything," I repeated.

Pilar glared at me and told my mother, "Mrs. Blume, it is not healthy."

"Well, you know these young people, Pilar," Mom said. "They like to be thin. It's fashionable." She smiled at me and said we should go shopping for a dress for the benefit. I reminded her of all the work we still have to do if there is going to *be* a benefit. And that I'd rather shop for a dress next week. (My new goal is to fit *comfortably* into a size two by then.)

I made loads of phone calls for Mom.

Better go back downstairs. If I'm with Mom, maybe she won't start drinking.

4:09 P.M.

I was too late. Mom started drinking at lunch. My staying home didn't make any difference on that score. After lunch she said she was tired and went to her room. I worked on the benefit alone. I only need three more items for the auction and we can have the program printed up. Hmm. Someone has to write all those items up. Better call the HCA office and see who can do it.

10:16 P.M.

Lost another pound.
I've reached my goal.
The skirt fits.
Why am I so nervous?

NERVES

Wired.
Tightly wound ~~wound tight?~~
And bound
To thoughts
That imprison.
My heart can't take wing
While I am bound

Here
On the ground
Tightly wound.

© Maggie Blume

Another depressing poem by Maggie Blume.

Whatever made me think I could write poetry?

I'm going to resign from the staff of *Inner Vistas* when we go back to school. How could I have thought I'd be editor someday?

I feel like I'll never write a good poem or song lyric again.

I'm a failure.

I can understand why Dad is disappointed in me. I'm disappointing myself.

I've decided not to wear my new skirt. It fits, but it makes me look fat. Amalia is going to come over tomorrow to help me pick out something from my closet.

Good night.

Bad night.

Saturday 7/25
6:30 P.M.

Justin is going to pick me up any minute now. I'm so nervous. Maybe writing in my journal will help me stay calm.

Mom had a major hangover this morning and was in no shape to talk on the phone. I handled benefit business for her. Lots of phone calls.

Amalia came over this afternoon to help me pick out what to wear tonight. I wish she hadn't bothered. She drove me crazy. For example, I put on my purple satin pants. "My hips look *huge* in these," I groaned.

"Are your crazy?" Amalia exclaimed. "They look great on you."

I hate it when people tell social lies just to make you feel better. Why wouldn't she admit that some of my clothes make me look fat? Whenever I said I was too fat for an outfit she'd contradict me. Then she got really serious. "I think you're dieting too much, Maggie," she said. "You look *so* thin it's not healthy."

I told her that I have tiny bones. That I'm supposed to be thin. She argued with me about that. She was pretty annoyed by the time she left. But not as annoyed as I am with her.

I decided to wear the brown skirt and velveteen top after all. I changed my nail polish from pink to

Uh-oh, Justin's here.

                              Sometime After Midnight
The good news is my date with Justin Randall is over.

Dad made sure he was home when Justin picked me up. I was afraid my parents would embarrass me. But they didn't. I don't think Justin could tell that Mom had been drinking. And Dad didn't ask him what his parents did for a living or remind him of my midnight curfew.

We made our escape pretty quickly.

Justin looked incredibly handsome and relaxed. I felt incredibly ugly and nervous. I didn't know what to say.

Once we got in the getaway car, he started a conversation by asking me how things were going with my new job. I told him about Little Guy and the photographs we took for the benefit. Then we talked about Vanish and some of our rehearsals. Justin does a great imitation of Rico.

By the time we reached the theater, I was more relaxed.

I was on a date with Justin Randall! And we were clicking.

People were lined up around the block for tickets to the film, but Justin already had ours so we breezed right in. He headed straight for the refreshment stand. "This is our first movie together," he said. "We have to have popcorn." He ordered two popcorns with butter without even asking me if I wanted one. I hate it when people do that.

"No butter or salt on one of those," I told the counter guy.

"But that's the best part," Justin protested.

"It's the way I like it," I said.

Justin shrugged his shoulders and handed me my popcorn.

The film was so good I don't think he noticed that I didn't eat anything. When I was tempted to have some popcorn, I would imagine the solid fat stuffed into the little holes of each kernel. I was determined not to eat anything until dinner. And I didn't.

After Maxie Benox's first number in the film, Justin put his arm around my shoulder and whispered in my ear, "See why I think you sound like her?"

He kept his arm around me until the film was over.

I wished that movie would go on forever.

As we were leaving the theater, someone shouted, "Hey, Justin."

Justin looked around and waved. "There's Frank," he said. He took my hand and we pushed through the crowd until we reached a group of seven Vista kids. I'd seen them around school but didn't know any of them. When we got outside, Justin introduced me. "Maggie's the lead singer in Vanish," he said.

A few of those kids were at the Battle of the Bands. They said they loved my singing. They don't know how I sound now and that I haven't written a new song in a month. That I probably never will.

"Come on over to the bowling alley with us," Frank said. "We're going to eat and roll a few."

I hoped Justin wouldn't accept. I've only bowled a few times. I knew that I would make a fool of myself.

"Can't," Justin told them. "We have a dinner reservation at Juanita's." He put his arm around my waist. I sucked in my breath so he wouldn't feel my roll of fat.

"Juanita's!" exclaimed Frank. "Way cool!"

"Have you ever been there?" Justin asked me.

I shook my head no. I'd heard of Juanita's and knew that it was a trendy Mexican restaurant.

"If it's your first time, order a Juanita's Burrito," someone said. "It's stuffed with rice, beans, chicken, and cheese. And they have the best salsa ever."

"And don't forget the guacamole," Frank added.

"All this food talk is making me hungry," said another guy. "Let's go."

They were gone and it was just Justin and me again. He had made dinner reservations and had turned down a chance for us to hang with his friends. This was a real date.

Juanita's was just around the corner from the theater. It was a good thing we had reservations. The place was mobbed.

We followed the maître d' past tables piled with plates of overstuffed burritos. How could one person eat all that food?

Our table was in a corner. We'd barely sat down when they brought us chips and salsa. Justin ordered guacamole. I *never* eat avocados. They taste great, but they are loaded with calories. And chips are greasy. I decided I wouldn't eat anything until the main course. I wasn't going to gain back all the weight I lost in one meal.

Justin tried to get me to order a fruit smoothie, but those are loaded with calories too. I saw one on another table. It looked amazing, but I had to show some RESTRAINT. I ordered a diet cola.

Juanita's was noisy and the air was heavy with food smells. It was hard to be heard without shouting.

The waiter handed us menus. "I think we know what we want," Justin said. He looked at me. "Juanita's Burritos, right?"

Wrong.

"I'd like to see what else they have," I said.

The waiter left and I scanned the menu. Justin told me all the great dishes he had eaten there. All fattening. How come he's not fat?

The waiter came back. "I'll have the house salad," I told him.

"And for your main course?" he asked.

"Just the salad," I explained. "You can bring it when he has his burrito."

"A house salad is really small," Justin said. "Don't you want anything else?"

"I like salad."

"Isn't there *any*thing else on the menu

you like? What about chicken chocolate mole? They're famous for that."

Chicken and chocolate? Was he crazy?

Justin was annoyed with me, like I had spoiled his good time because I didn't want to eat what he wanted me to eat. Since when is ordering a salad a crime? I was disappointed in Justin. I didn't know he was such a control freak.

"We have a Caesar salad," the waiter said. "That's more a dinner size. How about that?"

To calm Justin down, I agreed to the Caesar salad. But he still wasn't happy. As soon as the waiter left he made a comment about how Caesar salad was a weird thing to order in a Mexican restaurant. He added that it wasn't like I had to be on a *diet.* He said "diet" as if being on one were insane.

Justin drank his smoothie and ate chips, salsa, and guacamole. I ate a few chips so he would leave me alone. But he kept shoving the guacamole in my face. I finally ate a little on a chip. But only one.

I wish we hadn't gone out to dinner.

Justin was acting weird. This was *not* fun.

When my salad arrived it was dripping with dressing. Justin had made such a big fuss over my order that I had forgotten to ask for the dressing on the side.

He dove into his burrito and went on and on about how good it was. Of course he wanted me to "at least taste it."

I wouldn't.

I poked through my salad. Parmesan cheese stuck to the greasy dressing that stuck to the lettuce. It might as well have been deep-fried.

"Don't you like it?" Justin asked.

I took a bite. "It's good," I said.

I ate a few more bites while he continued to wolf down his meal. I made it through about a third of the salad, but I couldn't eat anymore. Why should I stuff myself just because he does? Of course he had to notice that I had stopped eating.

"Are you sick or something?" he asked.

"I'm just not very hungry," I said. "I don't have a big appetite."

"More like *no appetite*," he mumbled under his breath. I ignored that. I couldn't believe he was getting upset because of what I did or did not eat.

"You should have told me you don't like Mexican food," he said.

"It's not that. I'm just not very hungry tonight," I said. "It's no big deal. Stop making a big deal out of it."

"Well, you should have told me," he said again. He pushed away his plate with the half-eaten burrito. "It's no fun to go to a restaurant with someone who doesn't eat."

He signaled to the waiter. "I suppose you don't want dessert either."

"No. I don't. I never eat dessert."

Justin passed on dessert too.

We didn't say another thing to each other until we were outside.

The blast of fresh air felt good. As we walked down the block I could feel the waistband on my skirt shift from side to side. Three days ago it was snug and now it was loose. I felt thin and I knew I would be thinner. All it took was self-control.

I sighed.

I started to talk about the film again. But Justin didn't seem very interested in the film . . . or in me. He brought me home.

I have a feeling that our first date was also our last. Fine by me. I think Justin was looking for an excuse to pick a fight with me anyway. I'm way too ugly for him.

Sunday 7/26
6:05 P.M.

Boring day. Slept until noon. Still tired.

Dad's having a screening party here. I have to make an appearance. I hope I at least like the movie.

Amalia phoned around noon and left a message. I was here but I didn't pick up and I didn't call her back. She's going to want to know all about the date and that is the last thing I want to talk about. Amalia was more excited about it than I was. Maybe *she* should go out with him. Amalia likes to eat. They can try out all the restaurants in Palo City. Then they can move on to Anaheim.

Justin left a message too. "Maggie. It's Justin. About last night. I'm sorry about what I said at the restaurant. It's just that . . . you didn't seem to be having a very good time. . . . But, well, call me. Okay?"

Forget him.

Forget last night.

I have more important things to worry about.

There's my phone again.

6:15 P.M.

I should have let Zeke leave a message too. It was a mistake to pick up the phone. All he did was complain, complain, complain. I told him that if he stopped complaining and tried harder to have fun the time would go by faster. He shut up with the complaints after that. But he hung on the line and told me it was my turn. That I should say something.

"Like what?" I asked.

"I don't know. Like what did you do last night?"

I tried not to sigh too loudly.

"Nothing," I said. "Nothing important. I have to go. Dad's having this screening."

"I wish I could go to the screening. What's he showing?"

"I don't know. Good-bye, Zeke."

We hung up.

Zeke can really get on my nerves.

Monday 7/27
1:13 P.M.

Manning the front desk during lunch hour. Piper went out for lunch. Offered to bring me back something. Told her I brought lunch from home and I'd eat it here. That's not lying. It's none of her business what I eat or don't eat.

The people who volunteer here are always bringing in food for snacking — cakes, cookies — all fattening. I guess Piper is another one of those lucky people who can eat all they want without being fat.

I'm beginning to enjoy my diet. I feel clean, light, and in control.

I'm disgusted when I think of the mountains of cakes, cookies, and ice cream I used to eat.

1:30 P.M.

Phone call. I answered the way I usually do, "Palo City Animal Shelter. This is Maggie. Can I help you?"

"Well, that sounds very businesslike," said the male voice on the other end. My father. "I thought your job was to take care of the animals. What are you doing answering the phone?"

I explained that I was working at the front desk while the volunteer went for lunch.

"What about *your* lunch?" he asked.

I told him that I was eating at the desk and he made some lame joke about my terrible working conditions.

I didn't say anything and waited for him to tell me why he'd called.

"Your mother didn't show up for a benefit committee meeting," he said. "The HCA office called to see if I know where she is."

My heart sank. I didn't know where Mom was either. Dad and I were both thinking the same thing, but we didn't say it. Mom was off somewhere drinking. Was she going to blow this chance to regain her place in Hollywood high society?

"Seems like your mother has lost interest in the benefit," Dad said.

I agreed and told him that she also had a two o'clock meeting at HCA to go over the program for the auction one more time before it went to the printer.

Dad asked me if there was any way *I* could go over to the HCA office and cover for Mom.

"I'm working *here*," I reminded him.

"Those shelter people will let you leave," he said. "After all, the benefit is for them. They get the money."

I said I would tell Piper that Mom was shorthanded and needed my help. Dad said his car would pick me up in half an hour. He added that the success of the benefit is important to Mom. He said she'd been absent from the Hollywood social scene lately and that the benefit was her chance to return to it. "So do what you can, Maggie," he told me. "And let me know how I can help. We won't make a big deal out of it, but let's be there when your mother needs us."

"Okay, sure," I agreed.

After I hung up I realized that neither of us was surprised that Mom has disappeared. We didn't know where she was, but we knew what she was doing. And we knew that sooner or later she'd be home — drunk.

I hated to leave Piper with all of my work on top of her own. "Good thing I had a big lunch," was her parting comment.

I told the committee that Mom was sick and that I was supposed to have called to tell them. I apologized and we got down to work.

Mom never showed up at the HCA office. She came home a little while ago and went right to her room. I heard her mumbling to herself and then I heard ice clinking in her glass. I didn't bother to say hi. I'm too disappointed and mad. And worried about the benefit.

The program is ready for the printer. It was a good thing we checked it. There were a bunch of typing errors — like "Dinner for 40 at Top of the Hart," which was supposed to read Dinner for 4!

Two of the women on the committee, Janice and Lana, have known Mom for a long time. I bet they didn't believe my explanation for Mom's absence. Mom used to go to aerobics class with them. They were always doing things together. Once they went to this fancy health spa in the desert. Mom looked great when she came home. She had lost five pounds and looked really healthy.

Then she started drinking more and more and seeing her friends less and less. Once I heard Dad ask Mom about Janice and Lana and she said they were goody-goodies who didn't know how to have fun. Mom probably insulted them. She can be mean when she's been drinking.

She's lost a lot of friends because of her problem. I hope she doesn't lose more.

There's a message from Amalia on my machine reminding me that there's a Vanish practice tomorrow night. There is no way I can see Justin Randall. I left her a message saying that I can't go. I used the benefit as my excuse.

Diet going *very* well. I love this empty feeling.

Tired.

Very busy at shelter today. Mom here when I came home. Told her what we did at meeting yesterday. She thanked me for my help. Said she'd been working on benefit all afternoon, but it was giving her a headache and she had to get out of the house. She told Pilar she didn't want any dinner and left.

Dad still at work.

Pilar had cooked a big meal for us. When she saw that I was the only one home she asked me where I wanted to eat. I told her that I ate before I came home.

Now she's in a big snit about cooking for a family who never eats.

After she went to her room, I ate a small scoop of low-fat cottage cheese, a slice of cucumber, and one pretzel.

I've lost another pound.

Working at the shelter is getting on my nerves. The animals are okay, but Piper can be really bossy.

E-mail from Zeke. He has *not* stopped kvetching. Now he's complaining about the food at camp.

He wants me to e-mail him back and tell him what Pilar's been cooking for us.

FOOD. FOOD. FOOD.

WHAT'S WRONG WITH EVERYBODY?

CAN'T THEY THINK ABOUT ANYTHING ELSE?

Wednesday 7/29
6:09 P.M.

Four messages on my machine when I came home:

1. Zeke saying that I should check my e-mail and answer him.
2. Justin saying he was sorry I wasn't at the rehearsal and would I please call him.
3. Amalia saying same as Justin.
4. Dawn calling from Stoneybook. Said she misses me. Wondered how I was

and what was going on in Palo City.
She wants me to call her back too.

I don't feel like talking to anybody. Think I'll take a nap before dinner.

8:30 P.M.

Dinner started out on a bad note. Pilar was grumpy with me because I asked her not to put dressing on my salad or sauce on my grilled fish. Mom was drinking her dinner. And Dad was grumpier than Pilar.

I told Mom that the hotel called with some questions about the benefit dinner. Mom paid attention for a little while and I got the information I needed. I'll pass it on to Janice tomorrow and hopefully she'll take care of it.

I ate the salad and half the fish. For once, no one tried to make me eat more.

But Mom did notice how I looked. She scowled at me. "I thought we were going to do something about that hair."

"I got a haircut last week," I told her. "You said you liked it."

"Did I?" she asked. "Well, now it looks limp."

She poured herself more wine. Dad winced.

"What are you wearing to that blasted dinner?" Mom asked me.

I had been so busy I'd forgotten about buying a dress. The last thing I wanted to do was go shopping with my mother. When she's drinking, she can really embarrass me.

"I'll wear the outfit I wore to Dad's last premiere," I said. "Okay?"

"Fine. I'll just wear any old thing too."

"Why don't you two buy yourselves something special," Dad said. "And, Eileen, have a beauty day at the Hollywood Spa. It would be good for you."

I knew Dad was suggesting the spa because it would be hard for Mom to drink during a day of beauty treatments.

She glared at him. "How can I do that and manage the benefit? Sometimes you are very dense, Hayden."

My stomach churned. I wished I hadn't eaten the fish.

The front doorbell rang.

Pilar poked her head out from the kitchen. "Want me to get it?" she asked.

I jumped up and said I'd go.

Amalia was at the door.

I was surprised. She'd never just "dropped by" before. I gave her a big hello. Amalia has the most beautiful smiling face. It glows.

My father yelled, "Who is it?"

I yelled back that it was someone to see me. He came into the hall, said hi to Amalia, and told me that he was going back to the office. I asked him what Mom was doing and he said quietly, "She's gone out. Bring Amalia to the dining room for something to eat before Pilar cleans up." He smiled at Amalia. "Make Pilar's day and eat something, will you?"

"I already ate, Mr. Blume," she said. "But I might be able to help out in the dessert department."

We went into the dining room and Pilar

gave Amalia a huge piece of lemon tart and a glass of milk.

"Maggie used to love my lemon tarts," Pilar told Amalia. She turned to me. "But I suppose you don't want any tonight."

"No," I replied. "I don't."

I know I sounded rude, but I don't care. Pilar has to learn not to bug me about eating. I think she wants everyone to be fat like her.

While Amalia ate, she explained that she could only stay a half hour. That her mother dropped her off and would pick her up when she finished the family food shopping.

"I thought I'd stop by and see what's going on with you," she said. "You haven't answered any of my phone calls."

I told her I've been really busy. I asked Amalia how her job was going. She told me all about the ice-cream parlor. I've secretly vowed never to eat ice cream again.

Finally, Amalia finished her tart and we came up to my room. She threw herself across my bed and leaned on her elbows. "So tell me," she said excitedly. "How was your date with Justin?"

There was no way I was going to give Amalia or anyone else a blow-by-blow description of my disastrous night with Justin.

"It was all right," I said. "The film was really good. But I'm not that interested in Justin, not as a boyfriend."

Amalia looked surprised. "Does Justin know that?" she asked. "I mean, he was really disappointed that you weren't at the rehearsal."

"We'll still be friends," I told her.

I changed the subject by asking about the rehearsal. Amalia said that it didn't go very well. "It wasn't the same without you," she said. "You were missed."

Truth Translation: *Vanish needs a lead singer. Not necessarily me.*

"Rico said to remind you that they want some new material from you," Amalia added.

"I'm working on a song," I lied.

Truth Translation: *I know that Rico and the rest of the band are sick of my old songs. So what makes them think they'd like any new songs better?*

Amalia asked when I would be able to go back to rehearsals. I told her not until after the benefit. She said that she wouldn't schedule any rehearsals until I could be there.

"You still haven't told me what happened on the date or why you and Justin are 'just friends,'" Amalia said.

I just shrugged.

"Have you talked to him since Saturday?" she asked.

She wouldn't give up. I never realized that Amalia was so nosy.

"It's no big deal, Amalia. And I really don't want to talk about it. It's sort of boring."

Truth Translation: *Mind your own business.*

Amalia was quiet for a minute. I probably hurt her feelings. I hope she's learned a lesson about prying into other people's business.

I changed the subject by introducing her to Zeke's turtles.

She picked up Zeus and asked me, "Did you go out to eat or anything after the movie?"

I couldn't believe it. She wasn't giving up.

The doorbell rang.

Saved by the bell.

"That's probably your mother," I said.

I went downstairs with Amalia and said hello to Mrs. Vargas. She said what a great house we had and they left.

HOME

In this big house
I am alone
It's a prison
Not a home.

I can't stay here
I want to disappear.

Empty
Light

Free
That's how I want to be.

What a stupid poem.
I'm going to bed.
One more day until the benefit.
I'm not looking forward to it.
I'm not looking forward to anything.

Thursday 7/30
8:13 P.M.

What an awful day!

The only thing that's going well is my diet. Lost another pound. All my jeans are baggy on me. Yes! I have definitely gone down a size.

Dragged at work. Mom wasn't here when I came home.

I went to the kitchen. Pilar wasn't there.

A fresh loaf of bread was cooling on the counter and a chicken and vegetables were roasting in the oven. The bread smelled wonderful, but I had to ignore it. I wrote a note: *Pilar, I already had dinner. Maggie.*

Took some carrot sticks and low-fat cottage cheese from the fridge and brought them to my room.

9:12 P.M.

Tried to work on song lyrics about abandoned animals, but they were awful. My writing stinks.

Heard Dad come in around seven-thirty. He came up to my room and asked where Mom was. Told him I didn't know. He said dinner was ready. Told him I already ate.

11:04 P.M.

Mom still isn't home.

Last year Mom didn't come home at all one night. Dad acted like it wasn't a big deal and made up some story about how she probably had told him she was going someplace, but that he'd forgotten. He never forgets anything so I knew he was lying.

Neither of our parents were there when Zeke and I got up the next morning. Pilar made us go to school anyway.

When we came home, Dad was back, but Mom wasn't. He said that she was on a trip with Janice. He said she had called his office the day before to remind him that she was going on this trip, but his secretary had forgotten to give him the message. She would be home the next day.

Later I overheard Dad talking on the phone. He said, "Let her sleep it off, Janice, and I'll come for her in the morning. I want to keep it from the kids."

I wonder where Mom is now.

I wonder what excuse Dad will make up this time.

Friday 7/31
3:00 A.M.

Mom still isn't home.

Tried to sleep. No luck.

I went downstairs around midnight. Dad and Pilar were in the kitchen. I stopped at the closed door and listened before going in. Dad was telling Pilar that he was going out to look for Mom and that she should call the hospitals. I wonder if Pilar did that the last time Mom disappeared.

I pushed the door open. "Is there anything I can do?" I asked.

Dad seemed surprised. I saw the saddest look in his eyes. This time he didn't make up a story. He said that he was going to look for Mom, that he was sure he would find her, and that I should go to bed and get some rest.

MOTHER

Wanderer
Alone with a bottle.
Where will you go?

Wanderer
Alone with a bottle
Are you happy? ~~Don't you love us?~~

Mother
Alone in a bottle
Who do you love?

Not me.

Mother,
Where are you now?

I am alone.

© Maggie Blume

5:30 A.M.

Dad just came in with Mom. I heard him trying to get her to go up the stairs to her room. She was crying. Dad was telling her to keep quiet. She yelled that he should leave her alone.

What would have happened if he hadn't found her?

Mom not up this morning.

She was sleeping by the pool when I came home from work.

Work. What a disaster.

Piper noticed that I was tired this morning. She asked me if I was okay. I said I was fine. She said I looked pale. She was eating a bagel with cream cheese and offered me half.

Told her I wasn't hungry.

Which I wasn't.

She asked again if I was okay.

Doesn't anyone mind their own business?

Fed dogs. Put Laddie in run. Fed cats. Put another dog in run. Swept floor.

Suddenly Piper screamed from the back of the shelter, "Maggie, bring two leashes. Quick!"

I grabbed a couple of leashes. As I rushed toward the dog run I heard barking and snarling. Laddie and a black Lab were fighting. Piper was trying to separate them. "Stay there!" she yelled. "Throw me a leash."

I did. She managed to put it on the black Lab. Laddie ran to me. "Bring him in," Piper ordered.

I clipped on the other leash and led Laddie to his crate. A big tuft of hair was missing from his neck. I could see his skin, but he wasn't bleeding. Laddie lay down in his crate, put his chin on his folded paws, and looked up at me. His eyes were loving, not accusing.

Piper came in. She put the other dog in his crate. He growled at Laddie.

Laddie whimpered.

"Well, that was a pretty big mess," Piper scolded me. "Don't you know enough to clear the run before you put a new dog out?"

I was surprised that Piper was scolding me. Didn't *she* know how terrible I felt about what had happened?

"Sorry," I said. "I didn't do it on purpose."

"Of course you didn't do it on purpose. I just don't understand how you could make such a stupid mistake." She studied me. She still looked angry but her voice softened. "Are you okay?" she asked. "You always look so tired."

"I *told* you I'm okay."

Piper has some nerve to criticize how I look. She's not so great-looking herself.

"Give Laddie some water and come back to my office," she ordered. "I'm going to warm up some soup. I want you to eat something and take a break."

She headed for her office.

As I poured water for Laddie, I started to cry.

I couldn't stop.

I didn't want Piper nagging me about eating. And I didn't want her to see me crying. There was no way I was going to eat soup.

I was all tingly and nervous — like small electric shocks were going through me.

I couldn't stay in that place another minute.

I brushed the hair out of Laddie's eyes. He looked up at me sadly. "I'm sorry I let that dog out when you were in the run, Laddie," I said softly. "And I'm sorry about your hair." I patted him and said good-bye.

Then I walked out of the shelter.

Maybe Dad's right about me.

Maybe I *am* a quitter.

9:08 P.M.

Mom came out of her room from a "nap" at around four o'clock this afternoon. She didn't say anything about her disappearance last night. Neither did I.

Her face was puffy and she had big circles under her eyes, but she wasn't drinking. I told her there was a bunch of messages on her machine, reminded her that the benefit is tomorrow night, and asked if there was anything I could do to help.

"Oh, I suppose so." She sighed.

We checked the messages together. She said she had a splitting headache and asked me to go over to the HCA office and do a few things for her.

As we walked down the hall together she caught a glimpse of herself in the mirror and said sadly, "I look really awful." I looked at our side-by-side reflections. "I hope we both look a little better by tomorrow," she added.

Mom's right. I'm ugly. But at least I'm not fat anymore. And I'm going to be thinner. I may not be perfect, but I can try to look it.

Message from Zeke on my machine when I came back from HCA. More kvetching. I don't know why, but his message made me start to cry. I couldn't listen to the whole thing. I miss Zeke. But I'm glad he wasn't here for Mom's disappearing act last night.

Mom's in the family room now. I peeked in a little while ago. She was reading a magazine and drinking a glass of wine. I hope that's all she drinks tonight. It would be so embarrassing for Dad — me too — if Mom missed the benefit tomorrow.

I wonder what would be worse: Mrs.

Hayden Blume, HCA Benefit Chairperson, as a no-show. Or, Mrs. Hayden Blume, HCA Benefit Chairperson, shows up drunk.

I'm sick of the benefit.

I'm sick of life.

I'm going to bed.

Saturday 8/1
1:34 P.M.

Justin just called me on Mom's line. He said he called on the family line because I hadn't returned his calls and he wanted to be sure I was okay. "Are you sick?" he asked.

"No," I told him. I explained that I've been very busy with the benefit and my job. I didn't know what to say next. But he kept the conversation going by saying he'd missed me at the band practices.

"Maggie, are you not coming to band practice because of what happened at Juanita's?" he asked.

I didn't know what to say. What came out

was something like: "I wasn't feeling very well that night. I'm sorry."

"If you were sick, then *I'm* sorry," he said. "You had an upset stomach and I was pushing you to eat. I wish you had told me."

"That's okay," I assured him. I liked that he said he was sorry, even if his apology was based on a fake upset stomach.

I was thinking Justin and I might try again. But then he ruined everything by saying we should go back to Juanita's another time, when I can enjoy the food.

I didn't bother to tell him that I'll *never* enjoy the food at Juanita's.

Why can't people go on dates without making such a big deal about food?

There was another call on my mother's line. It was the HCA office with a last-minute question about the benefit. I told Justin I had to go. I was relieved to have an excuse to end the call.

Now that I'm writing about the phone call, I realize that Justin *had* to call me. The band doesn't like rehearsing without a lead singer, and we have a gig next Saturday night. Justin wanted to make sure he wasn't the reason I wasn't going to band rehearsals.

Amalia probably told him to call.

If I just skip a few more rehearsals, maybe they'll replace me. I hope so. Justin can take the new Vanish singer to Juanita's and they can stuff themselves to their hearts' content.

Feeling wonderfully thin today. I fit into a size-two black lace minidress that was tight two months ago. Now it's loose.

Had handful of dry cereal and some grapefruit juice for breakfast. Won't eat again until benefit.

Mom still sleeping. At least she's home.

Dad went into office for a couple of hours. Asked me to keep an eye on Mom.

Be glad when tonight is over.

5:29 P.M.

Mom got up around two. She took a long swim and showered. Then her masseuse came and gave her a massage and a facial. After that, her hairdresser came to do her nails, hair, and makeup. "I feel like a new woman," she told me. She looks it too. She's a beautiful woman — when she's not drinking.

The hairdresser blew out my hair. I don't look like a new woman. I look like the same sloppy, dull Maggie. I put on the black lace minidress, but it doesn't look right. And the outfit I bought for my date with Justin isn't dressy enough. Mom was right. I should have bought a new outfit. Now I'm wearing the dress I wore to the premiere of Dad's last film. It's longer than I remember. Too long. Nothing I can do about it now. We're leaving for the benefit in ten minutes.

As far as I can tell, Mom hasn't had a drink all day. I'm keeping my fingers crossed that it stays that way.

11:30 P.M.

The benefit's over. Finally.
I could tell Mom was nervous when she

and Dad and I met in the front hall to go out to the limo. Dad said Mom looked beautiful. "What difference does it make?" she replied. "The benefit's going to flop. That's what they get for scheduling it the same night as three other benefits."

Dad said something about it not having to be a flop. Mom turned her back on him and walked out the door while he was still talking.

By the time Dad and I climbed into the limo, Mom had opened the car bar and was dropping ice into a tumbler of scotch.

Dad sat across from her. "I don't think it's a good idea to drink before the evening begins, Eileen, dear. Do you?"

Mom took a gulp of her drink and said sarcastically, "Hayden, *dear*, I think it's a splendid idea."

I didn't want to be in the limo. I didn't want to go to the benefit. I didn't want to be with my parents. I thought, *I could just jump out right now and run into the house. They can't make me go.* Then I pictured the animals in the shelter and Laddie's loving, trusting eyes. I had been working on the benefit too. I had to go. Especially if Mom was drinking.

And drink she did.

When she poured her second drink, Dad said, "Eileen, I want you to stop this *right now*."

Mom kept pouring and replied, "Hayden, I want you to mind your own business *right now*."

As I wrote that, I had the strangest thought. Did I sound like that when Justin was trying to get me to eat? No. I was angry, but I didn't yell. Besides, Mom and drinking is the opposite of me and eating. Mom is out of control. I'm taking control of my life. She's doing something that's bad for her. I'm doing something that's good for me.

I just wish I hadn't been so rude to Justin. Even if he was pushing me to eat, I didn't have to bark at him.

By the time Mom was pouring her third drink, Dad couldn't even look at her. He complained about L.A. traffic and wondered if there was any way to get us to the hotel faster. We pulled up in front of the hotel as Mom finished her fourth drink.

As I climbed out of the limo behind Dad I heard him say to himself, "I'm going to have that bar taken out."

"You should have done it a long time ago," I mumbled.

I know he heard me. His back stiffened, but he didn't say anything.

When we walked into the hotel, Dad headed over to a big producer buddy of his and Mom headed for the bar.

I looked around. The dog and cat posters were hanging just the way I had imagined them. "They look perfect," a friendly voice said. It was Janice. Lana was behind her. They told me I looked beautiful.

"You've lost some weight," said Lana. "It's becoming."

At that moment I was incredibly proud of myself. This was my reward for not eating a greasy Juanita's Burrito. At least I can do something right.

"Where's your mother?" Janice asked.

I didn't want to tell Mom's friends that

my mother had gone straight to the bar, so I said I didn't know.

Janice said I had been a great help with the benefit.

"You've done a lot of filling in for your mother," added Lana. "We're really grateful to you."

I wondered if they'd still be friends with Mom after the benefit.

As they went off to look for Mom, I heard Janice say, "She's a nice girl but . . ."

I couldn't hear the rest, but it's easy to imagine. "She's a nice girl, but too bad she's so unattractive."

The next person I saw was Piper. She was standing with a friendly-looking dark-haired man and pointing to the poster of Laddie. I had the happy thought that he might adopt Laddie.

When the man left, I ran to Piper. "Laddie's photo looks great," I said. "Was that man interested in adopting him?"

"I don't know," she said. And walked away.

I felt awful. I wished I could disappear.

I saw one of the volunteers from the shelter head in my direction. I hid behind a big plant before he spotted me. After he passed by, I decided to get a diet soda. As I headed toward the bar, I noticed that Mom was there. I gave up the soda idea fast.

I looked around and wondered what I should do next. There was another half hour of mingling before dinner and the auction.

I noticed Dad with a group of his buddies. He signaled for me to join them. But I didn't want to listen to him schmoozing. And I certainly didn't want to be the subject of his bragging. *Maggie is a great musician. Next time you come by she'll play for you.*

I caught Dad's eyes and pointed to the other side of the hall, as if I had something important to take care of.

I did. I had to avoid Piper, who was coming toward me.

I pushed through a crowd of gorgeous, glamorous people and made my way to a corner of the room. But Piper had followed me.

"I'm sorry I walked away before," she said.

Why was *she* apologizing to *me*? *I* was the one who had walked out on *her*.

"I'm sorry about yesterday," I told her. Tears came to my eyes. I couldn't help it.

Don't cry, I ordered myself. *Don't cry.*

And I didn't.

"I came down on you pretty hard," Piper said. "But I'm worried about you, Maggie. You seem to be losing a lot of weight awfully fast. Have you been dieting? You might want to talk to someone — a doctor, or a counselor — about it. They can be a big help."

I wanted to tell Piper to mind her own business. But I couldn't. Not when she was trying to be nice to me even though I hadn't been nice to her. "I've been watching what I eat," I replied.

A waiter approached us with a tray of cheese sticks — one of my *former* food passions. They smelled good. Piper took a bunch. "We can share these," she said as she piled them on a napkin.

They smelled familiar and good.

I hadn't eaten since breakfast and I was hungry. I thought, *If I eat a cheese stick I'll have to eat less at dinner. But that's okay. Mom said the hotel food was terrible. I'd rather have a cheese stick than a piece of overcooked chicken.*

I reached for a cheese stick. As I was about to pick it up, another thought came into my head. *Cheese sticks are fattening. If I eat one, my diet will be over. I'll gain back all the weight I lost.*

I dropped my hand by my side and looked up.

Piper was staring at me.

I guess I had been looking at the cheese sticks and thinking about them for awhile.

"Are you sure you don't want one?" she asked in a soft voice. She sounded so kind.

I almost blurted out, *I do want one, but I can't. I just can't do it.*

But that would have made me sound like an idiot.

"Piper Klein," a voice called.

An elderly woman was hurrying toward us. "I've been looking all over for you."

"A big-time donor," Piper whispered in my ear. "I have to go."

She handed me the napkin of cheese sticks and was gone. When a waiter passed me with a tray of empty glasses I put the cheese sticks on the tray and hid in the bathroom until dinner.

At long last the lights dimmed, and people began finding their seats in the dining room. Mom sat at the head table. I sat with Dad and some people he hoped would invest in his next film project. Dad noticed I didn't eat my salad (too much dressing) or the potatoes, which were drowning in cream sauce. He said I wasn't eating enough lately and that my dress was hanging on me. I told him that I would buy some new clothes that fit. He said that wasn't the point.

I don't get it. He wants me to look perfect so he can show me off to his friends. Then he criticizes me for losing weight.

I decided he was upset about Mom and taking it out on me.

Before the auctioneer started the auction, Mom made a speech thanking her committee. Unless you knew her, you wouldn't know she'd been drinking. To me she sounded half asleep. She also tripped a little on her way back to her table. I thought I heard Dad mumble, "Close call."

People spent a lot of money on the auction items. The benefit was a success. Thanks to everyone on the benefit committee, except Mom.

The ride home was awful. Mom poured herself another drink. Dad picked up the phone and made a couple of business schmooze calls. But the three of us didn't say a word to one another all the way home.

I was glad Zeke wasn't there. For his sake.

Everything is so confused in my mind. I know it's wrong, but I'm beginning to hate my parents.

At home Dad went to his room and I came up here to mine. Mom is still downstairs. I'm sure she's drinking.

I hate it here.

And I hate myself.

I don't know where to begin. I've been crying for hours. If I write maybe I can finally stop.

I know it's just a statue, but it meant so much to me.

I have one of the wings on my desk. The rest of the statue is in tiny pieces.

I'm going to try to write down what happened from the beginning.

I was still awake when I heard a big crash from the family room. I knew Mom was down there drinking. I was afraid she'd hurt herself, so I ran out of my room.

Dad had heard the crash too. He pushed past me on the stairs to get to the family room first.

When I got there I saw the broken statue and Mom staggering around. There were broken pieces everywhere.

"The angel statue!" I cried. "You broke it."

"What was that stupid thing doing in the middle of the room anyway?" she slurred.

What Mom was calling "that stupid thing" was my favorite thing in the whole house. Sometimes, when I was a little kid and upset about something, I would talk to the angel.

Now the angel and child were in a thousand pieces on our family room floor.

"Eileen!" my father shouted. "Don't move. You'll cut your feet."

Mom was in her stocking feet. Dad's feet were bare. I was wearing slippers with hard soles.

"I'll get her," I told him.

"Be careful, Maggie," he said.

I stepped carefully through the glass and reached for my mother.

She told me to leave her alone.

"There's glass everywhere," I told her. "You'll hurt yourself. Let me help you."

"Get ahold of yourself, Eileen," my fathered ordered, "or I'll call the police."

My mother laughed at my father. It was a

horrible laugh. But she let me guide her to the bar stool.

She sat down and I went to the closet for a broom.

My father shook a finger in my mother's face. "This has gone too far. You'd better straighten yourself out, Eileen."

"I'll tell you what I'd better do, you cold fish," she said. "I'd better have another drink."

She reached for a bottle that was on the bar. He grabbed it away.

"I'm not going to let you destroy yourself," he said in a controlled, angry voice. "Or this family. It's time you admit that you have a serious problem."

"I DO NOT HAVE A PROBLEM!" she shouted.

She got off the stool and left the room.

I thought my father would run after her, but instead he turned to me. "And you," he said in the same angry voice. "I don't even know you anymore. Quitting jobs left and right. And not eating. This crazy dieting has to stop. You have a problem too, young lady."

"I don't have a —" I began to say.

I stopped myself. That was what my mother said about her drinking. And she has a problem. But I'm not like my mother. Or at least I never want to be.

I didn't know what to say to my father, so I didn't say anything.

He was staring at me as if I were a stranger. "What happened to my beautiful, talented, kindhearted daughter?" he asked sadly. "What's happening to my family?"

I was really angry at my mother at that moment — I still am — for making Dad so sad. But what bothers me more is that I'm disappointing him too.

I used to feel that I could make up for some of Mom's shortcomings, that I could be better than her. That I could make Dad happy. Now I know that I can never be good enough for him.

Dad suddenly exclaimed, "She must have a bottle in her room." As he ran from the room he told me to leave the mess, that Pilar would clean it up in the morning.

But I didn't leave it for Pilar. I wanted to

sweep up the remains of the angel and child myself. It was a ritual of respect for all that that statue had meant to me.

I started crying when I picked up the angel wing.

I'm still crying.

The phone woke me up a little while ago. I listened to the answering machine to find out who was calling me so early in the morning.

"Hey, Maggie," said the voice. "What's going on? Why don't you write to me? Why don't you call me? I know you're there. Pleeease pick up."

It was Zeke. I suddenly missed him very much. I wanted to talk to him.

As I picked up the receiver, I reminded myself that he was just a little kid. That I shouldn't let him know how bad things are at home. And, most of all, that he shouldn't come home. He was much better off at camp.

I said hi. Then I told him that I hadn't answered his e-mail or phone messages because I was really busy with the benefit.

He said he wished he'd been there and wanted me to tell him about it.

"Zeke Blume," I said, "you hate benefits. How come you're so interested in this one?"

He hesitated and then said, "Well, you know, because of how Mom got after that run in the rain last year. Remember?"

"Yeah," I said. "I remember."

I felt tears gather in my eyes again. I missed Zeke. I wanted so much to talk to him about what had happened last night. But he's my little brother and I also wanted to protect him.

Should I tell him? I didn't know what to do.

"Maggie," he said in a scared voice. "Are you there?"

"I'm here."

"Oh," he said with a sigh of relief. "I thought you'd hung up on me."

If I were Zeke and Zeke were me, would I

want him to tell me about Mom? I knew the answer was yes.

"Well, Mom's been drinking again, Zeke," I said.

"That's what I was afraid of," he said in a sad voice.

"I want to come home, Maggie," he said. "Tell Dad. Tell him he has to let me come home or else —"

I interrupted him. "Zeke, camp will be over in a week. We'll all be here when you come home. And the problems will be here too."

"Problem*s*?" he said. "What else is going on? You mean, like Dad being gone all the time?"

"Yes. And I sort of have a problem too."

I realized as I said it that I do have a problem. Not a huge problem. But a problem.

"What kind of problem?" Zeke asked in a small voice.

"An eating problem," I said. "It's hard for me to eat after being on a diet. I'm a little confused about food."

"Do you have that thing where people get really skinny?" he asked. "That 'ant-or-ex' thing."

I didn't want to say the word out loud. So I didn't correct Zeke's pronunciation. I just said, "It's not a huge problem. Anyway, I just want to say that I miss you, Zeke. And I am glad that you'll be home soon."

"I shouldn't have gone to camp," he said.

I realized that my eleven-year-old brother thought that if he hadn't gone to camp, he could have kept Mom from being a drunk, Dad from being an absent husband and father, and me from staying on a diet too long.

"Oh, Zeke," I pleaded, "don't, for even an instant, think you can keep bad things like this from happening. I was here. I couldn't keep Mom from drinking. We're not miracle workers. We're just kids."

"I guess. But I can help you, Maggie. I know I can."

"You can help me by staying at camp," I told him. "And then coming home and being the great brother you've always been."

"Can I call you every day until I come home?" he asked.

"Every day," I said.

I heard reveille being played at the tennis camp. It was the trumpet signal to wake up the campers. My brother, who hates to get up in the morning, had snuck out of his cabin early to call me.

"You better go," I said. "Before they think a bear stole you in the night."

"Okay. I'll call you tomorrow morning. Same time."

"Same time," I agreed.

"And Maggie, I'll tell you a secret."

"What?"

Zeke whispered into the receiver. "I sort of like tennis."

"Thanks for telling me," I said with a laugh. "How about dancing?"

"Yuck!" he shrieked.

I was smiling through tears when I hung up the phone.

Our family may have a lot of problems. But Zeke isn't one of them.

BROKEN (WINGS)

How do angels
know when you need them?
Do they stay and watch your every move
Or are they on call?

Did I forget
to call you, angel?
I didn't know I was in danger
that I was becoming a stranger
To myself.

Now you are gone.
I hold your broken wing
and wish you could be whole again.
A child's wish.

If I don't have my angel
Who will save me?

I think I'll work on that poem. It'll never be a song lyric. Too personal. But it expresses how I feel.

Ann M. Martin

About the Author

ANN MATTHEWS MARTIN was born on August 12, 1955. She grew up in Princeton, NJ, with her parents and her younger sister, Jane.

Although Ann used to be a teacher and then an editor of children's books, she's now a full-time writer. She gets the ideas for her books from many different places. Some are based on personal experiences. Others are based on childhood memories and feelings. Many are written about contemporary problems or events.

All of Ann's characters are made up. But some of her characters are based on real people. Sometimes Ann names her characters after people she knows, other times she chooses names she likes.

In addition to California Diaries, Ann Martin has written many other books, including the Baby-sitters Club series. She has written twelve novels for young people, including *Missing Since Monday, With You or Without You, Slam Book,* and *Just a Summer Romance.*

Ann M. Martin does not live in California, though she does visit frequently. She lives in New York with her cats, Gussie, Woody, and Willy. Her hobbies are reading, sewing, and needlework — especially making clothes for children.

Look for #9

Amalia, Diary Two

9/23, study hall

Nbook, you are not going to believe what magazine I have in front of me.

Teen'zine.

I hate Teen'zine. 99% of the articles are about guys and zits. ("How to Tell Them Apart" might be a useful piece.)

Anyway, I find it in the periodical rack as I'm avoiding h.work. And my eye catches a title on the cover, right under "Where Your Favorite Celebs Shop" and "Banish That Blemish":

You Don't Have an Eating Disorder—
But Your Friend Does

Well, maybe. I can't hu
about Maggie.

I'm leafing through the article. It's
full of headings and subheadings and
testimonials from kids who have "survived"
all these disorders.

Extreme ones. Anorexics who have
almost starved themselves. Bulimics who
wrecked their digestive systems from
throwing up too much.

I read about "binge-eating disorder,"
plain out-of-control eating. "Anorexia
athletica," when you stop eating because
you're preoccupied with exercise. "Night-
eating syndrome," when you starve during
the day but binge-eat at night. "Nocturnal
sleep-related disorder," when you don't
eat during the day but eat in a half-
sleep, half-awake state.

Suddenly I feel very full.

The article's pretty hopeful, though. It
talks about successful treatment, kids
who've gone on to lead normal lives, etc.

My thoughts return to Maggie. Is she
anorexic?